I · BELIEVE · IN · UNICORNS

by

BOB STANISH

Illustrated by Nancee Volpe

ISBN #0-916456-51-X

Printing No. 987

Good Apple, Inc.
Box 299
Carthage, IL 62321

I • BELIEVE • IN • UNICORNS

ACKNOWLEDGEMENTS

The author wishes to thank D.O.K. Publishing Company for permission to reprint the SCAMPER techniques, from SCAMPER, by Bob Eberle.

In addition, acknowledgement is given to:

Marge Frank, for her support, suggestions and the title.

Troy Cole, for the FOREWORD letter.

Dr. Norma Button and Dr. Cliff Barton, Gifted Program Coordinators of the Clear Creek Independent School District of League City, Texas and their staffs, for their field testing of the materials.

believe in Unicorns...

because magic-izing stretches minds
dreaming stimulates the creation of new worlds
fantasizing unleashes floods of inventions
wondering challenges ideas to multiply
supposing opens passageways to possibilities
and imagining ignites explosions of understanding

because believing in unicorns sparks and expands the skills of creative thinking,
SKILLS that kids need...
for making daily decisions
for solving problems
for keeping fresh, alert minds
for coping with and enjoying LIFE!

I BELIEVE IN UNICORNS is for nurturing creative thought. The activities are designed to develop and strengthen the four creative thinking processes:

FLUENCY..........the production of a large **number** of ideas, products or plans

FLEXIBILITY.....the production of ideas or products that show a **variety** of possibilities or realms of thought

ORIGINALITY....the production of ideas that are unusual and unique

ELABORATION..the production of ideas that display intensive detail or enrichment

All of the experiences are motivators: ideas which can spark exploration and application of possibilities. The thinking processes encouraged by these pages certainly can and will spill over into other areas of learning in your students' lives.

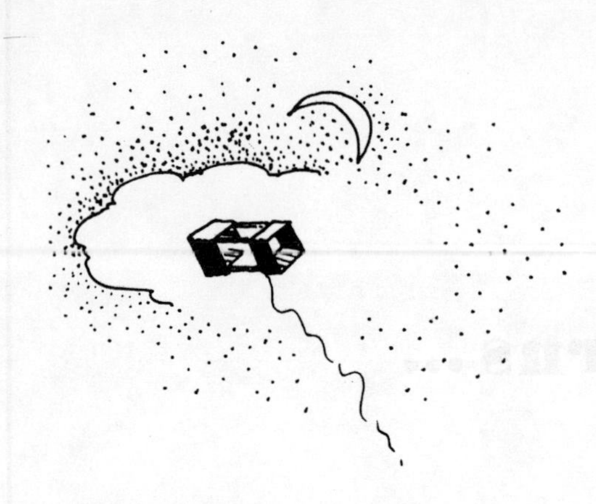

DEDICATION

This book is dedicated to Pat, Jon, Lindley, Mary G., Bert, two Jim's, David, Diane and Leah. It is also dedicated to wayward kites and unicorns - wherever they may be.

Dear Bob,

I now believe in unicorns, too. I believe they dwell very near misty mountain tops and deep in dew-draped dells. I know they are near when I discover a tiny mouse trail in fresh fallen snow or I meander with floats of gossamer on a soft autumn breeze.

Bob, because of your persistent belief in unicorns, you set forth to share it with others. In this sharing, you take them on a learning journey through lands with unicorns nearby. If they dare to come along on this adventure, they too, perchance, will glimpse a unicorn of their very own.

Best of all, you invite all of us to bring our children along. I shall. I hope others will too.

Troy Cole

TABLE OF CONTENTS

How to use this book...

This book was meant to be torn apart! Each STUDENT ACTIVITY page is designed for duplication so that it can be used by individuals or the entire class. The pages may be used by students working alone or in a teacher-directed setting. For the fullest development of creative thinking, it is recommended that the teacher be involved as a catalyst often.

Mix these activities in with other classroom learning projects. A workable plan is to use one or two a week, spread throughout the school year. Make sure that each activity is initiated when there is plenty of time for its completion, since the structure purposely seeks to generate lots of possibilities for consideration and expression.

Most of the adventures can involve writing. However, it is important that open-ended discussion and brainstorming be frequently incorporated into these activities. Combine the written and the oral expression as fits the needs and interests of your group.

A TEACHER PAGE accompanies each student page. Every teacher page outlines the following sections:

THE CREATIVE THINKING SKILLS--one or more of the creativity factors is the focus of each activity. There is no specific sequence for the pages or skills; they may be used in any order.

GETTING STARTED--some guidelines for approaching and beginning the activity, plus some motivators for loosening expression of ideas.

UPON COMPLETION--directions for how to share and evaluate the students' responses.

WHAT ELSE AND MORE--techniques for broadening the idea, following up on the results, adapting the process to an entirely different topic, or directing students' thinking in related but new directions.

The teaching suggestions are "starters" for you, just as the student suggestions are for them. Your use of them is optional. You are definitely encouraged to expand them, add to them, revise or steer responses into unexplored channels.

You will also find on each page a CREATIVE TEACHING TIP. These should provide for you a valuable collection of reminders and challenges to remember, consider and apply as you strive to promote the expression and expansion of creativity.

I BELIEVE IN UNICORNS is sprinkled with some strategies for affirming feelings and nurturing sensitivity to self, to others and to valuing situations in students' lives. The book offers creative ways to explore feeling, as well as thinking, because the author's experience has convinced him that knowledge grows more vigorously, and is employed most meaningfully, when combined with human sensitivity.

The activities in this book will expand YOUR creative thinking skills,too! Please do the creating along with your students. YOUR participation in the experience will add dignity and heighten enthusiasm for the idea, YOUR contributions to the sharing of products will illustrate the thinking processes to students, and YOUR stretching of your mind will make you a better teacher of creative thinking!

STEPS TOWARD CREATIVITY

What follows are some learning tips for teachers. Each STEP suggests some approaches or outlines techniques that will help you make the best use of this book AND will sharpen your skills as an instigator of the creative processes.

Step 1 WATCH YOUR QUESTIONS!

Questions can be frightening or exciting, intimidating or stimulating, expanding or restricting. It all depends on HOW they are asked! Here are some kinds of questions that can facilitate the UNICORN strategies:

OPEN-ENDED QUESTIONS have no one "right" response, but a multitude of answers. Ask questions such as: *"What if... the oceans were made of honey?" "... people had four legs?" "the sky was green?"*
Keep in mind these beginnings and use them to stimulate discussion in any academic area: "How many ways can you think of to...?" "What would you do if...?" "What might happen when...?" "In what other situations could...?"

FEELING QUESTIONS encourage students to examine their values and emotions. Here are some samples that you can use to start expression of feelings and beliefs: *"How do you feel when?" "How can you explain the way you felt about...?" "Can you remember another time when you felt the same way?" "What 'ing' words would you use to describe your reaction to...?" "Which is more important, _________ or ________?"*

ASSOCIATIVE QUESTIONS provide a stimulus for looking at ideas or things from many different sides. For example: *"How is a teaspoon like a smile?" "What could a can opener be used for besides opening cans?"*

Remember that YOUR response to students' answers is important! Try to be as open and accepting as possible, and allow lots of time for thinking!

Step 2 BRUSH UP ON BRAINSTORMING!

Brainstorming is a group method of generating a quantity of ideas in a short period of time. Here are some suggestions for effective brainstorming with your group:

1. ACCEPT EVERYTHING! Withhold criticism or evaluation of the ideas. They can be censored or refined later.
2. WELCOME THE OUTLANDISH! New ideas are born only when the freedom to hatch them exists. Encourage the wild and different!
3. DON'T STOP TOO SOON! Quantity is important, because the greater the number of ideas generated, the more likely is the occurrence of the unusual.
4. YOU PARTICIPATE TOO! When students are brainstorming, the teacher should contribute, as well. Your addition to the pool of ideas can demonstrate divergence and add excitement to the process.
5. BUILD and COMBINE WITH "OLD" IDEAS! It is valuable to brainstorm ways that existing ideas can be bettered, or to gather possibilities for combining two or more ideas into a third idea.

Step 3 TEACH YOUR KIDS TO SCAMPER!

Scamper, from *Scamper,* a book by Bob Eberle, is a list of the kinds of thinking and doing activities which spur ideas. Eberle has taken Alex Osborn's ideas from APPLIED IMAGINATION and rearranged them in a list that's easy to remember! Make sure you include these kinds of processes in your classroom.

S	SUBSTITUTE	Have a thing or person act or serve in the place of another.
C	COMBINE	Bring together or unite.
A	ADAPT	Adjust to suit a condition or purpose.
M	MODIFY	Alter or change the form or quality.
	MAGNIFY	Enlarge or make greater in quality or form.
	MINIFY	Make smaller, lighter, slower, less frequent.
P	PUT TO OTHER USES	Use for purposes other than the one originally intended.
E	ELIMINATE	Remove, omit, get rid of a quality, part or whole.
R	REVERSE	Place opposite or contrary to original position, or to turn it around.
	REARRANGE	Change order or adjust, make a different plan, adapt a layout or scheme.

Step 4 GIVE YOUR CLASSROOM A CLIMATE CHECK

The classroom environment is the soil for cultivation of creativity. These are some of the classroom conditions conducive to promoting creative thinking and creative expression:

Good Questioning Techniques Use open-ended questions rather than "right answer" questions. Provide problems that are unsolved. Ask students to test and challenge answers. Present questions which have no answers.

Self-directed Activity Encourage students' efforts to go beyond the assigned topic. Push them to expand the boundaries of the ideas.

Openness Respect, accept and delight in unusual ideas, unique directions or outlandish questions.

Stimulating Materials Provide a variety of enriching and exciting resources for stimulating inquiry.

Thinking Time Allow time for playing, experimenting, testing, and questioning. Students need time to fool around with ideas without the pressure to "get the right answer."

Idea Testing Offer opportunities for comparing, evaluating, examining and criticizing of divergent possibilities.

Freedom for Supposing Create situations which allow for guessing, posing possibilities and predicting outcomes with or without evidence.

Reinforcement Reward creative thinking with praise and encouragement. Without formal evaluation, assign value and prestige to unusual thoughts.

Step 5 INVENTORY CREATIVE THINKING

As students play with ideas and venture into activities such as those in this book, stop from time to time for an inventory of progress. As the year goes along, they should evidence growth in flexible, fluent, original and elaborative thinking.

One way to measure creative development is to use a method of checking, such as the CREATIVE SCORING GUIDE provided on the next page. Select an activity or a group of activities which accommodate all four factors of creative thinking. Duplicate the GUIDE, so that there is one for each student. Use the GUIDE to score each of the four areas. (The students can do this, themselves.) Make sure you date the sheet. Repeat the process monthly, and ask students to compare the scores with the previous asssessment. The scores may serve as a guide for you to direct your planning of future activities in creative thinking. One month's assessment can also act as a reminder to a student to work toward developing one of the skills in the upcoming activities.

CREATIVITY SCORING GUIDE

NAME ______________________________

ACTIVITY TITLE (s)______________________________

TODAY'S DATE______________________________

FLUENCY SCORE

In the box, write the total number of your ideas or responses.

FLEXIBILITY SCORE

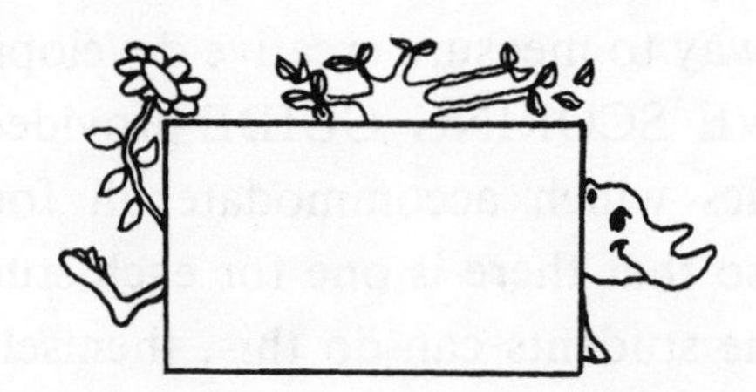

Count the number of **different** ideas (the different kinds or categories of ideas). Write the number in the box.

ORIGINALITY SCORE

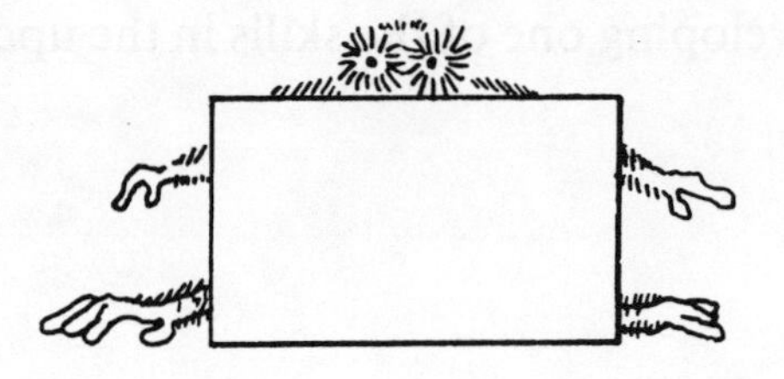

Count the number of ideas or answers you had that nobody else in this class had. Write that number in the box.

ELABORATION SCORE

Look for the ideas that are very descriptive, or the answers that have lots of interesting details. Count them and write the number in the box.

A FEW SELECTED REFERENCES

Bach, Richard, *Jonathan Livingston Seagull.* New York: Macmillan, 1970.

Barron, Frank, *Creativity and Personal Freedom.* New York: Van Nostrand Reinhold, 1968.

Bloom, Benjamin S., and David R. Krathwohl, *Taxonomy of Educational Objectives, Handbook 1: The Cognitive Domain.* New York: David McKay Company, Inc. 1956.

Borton, Terry, *Reach, Touch and Teach.* New York: McGraw-Hill Book Company, 1970.

Briggs, Dorothy, *Your Child's Self-esteem: The Key to His Life.* Garden City, N.Y.: Doubleday, 1970.

Brown, George I, *Human Teaching for Human Learning.* San Francisco: Esalen Institute, 1971.

Bruner, Jerome, *On Knowing.* New Haven, Conn.: Harvard University Press, 1962.

Combs, Arthur, and Snygg, Donald. *Individual Behavior,* rev. ed. New York: Harper & Row, 1959.

Cullum, Albert, *The Geranium on the Windowsill Just Died but Teacher You Went Right On.* New York: Quist, 1971.

Eberle, Bob, and Rosie Emery Hall, *Affective Education Guidebook: Classroom Activities in the Realm of Feelings.* Buffalo, New York: D.O.K. Publishers, Inc. 1975.

Eberle, Robert F., *Scamper: Games for Imagination Development.* Buffalo, New York: D.O.K. Publishers, Inc. 1971.

Fromm, Erich, *The Art of Loving.* New York: Harper & Row, 1956.

Getzels, J.W., and Jackson, P.W., *Creativity and Intelligence.* New York: Wiley, 1962.

Gordon, Thomas, *Parent Effectiveness Training.* New York: Wyden, 1970.

Gordon, William J.J., *Synectics.* New York: Harper and Row Publishers, 1961.

Greenberg, H.M., *Teaching with Feeling.* Indianapolis, Ind.: Pegasus, 1970.

Greer, Mary, and Rubenstein, Bonnie, *Will the Real Teacher Please Stand Up.* Pacific Palisades, Calif.: Goodyear, 1972.

Guilford, J.P., *The Nature of Human Intelligence.* New York: McGraw Hill Book Company. 1967.

Harris, Thomas, *I'm OK--You're OK.* New York: Harper & Row, 1969.

Kohl, Herbert R., *The Open Classroom.* New York: Random House, New York Review, 1970.

Krathwohl, David R., and Benjamin S. Bloom and Bertram B. Masia. *Taxonomy of Educational Objectives, Handbook ii: The Affective Domain,* David McKay Company, Inc. 1964.

Laliberte, N., *One Hundred Ways to Have Fun with an Alligator, or 100 Art Projects.* Blawvelt, N.Y.: Art Education Inc., 1969.

Lyon, Harold C. Jr., *Learning to Feel - Feeling to Learn.* Columbus, Ohio: Charles E. Merrill Publishing Company. 1971.

Meeker, Mary Nacol, *The Structure of Intellect: Its Interpretations and Uses.* Columbus, Ohio: Charles E. Merrill Publishing Company. 1969.

Osborn, Alex F., *Applied Imagination,* 3rd ed. New York: Charles Scribner's Sons. 1963.

Parnes, Sidney J., and Harold F. Harding (editors), *A Source Book for Creative Thinking,* Part Two, The Creative Process, Philosophy and Psychology of Creativity. New York: Charles Scribner's Sons. 1962.

Parnes, Sidney J., *Creative Behavior Guidebook.* New York: Charles Scribner's Sons. 1967.

Renzulli, Joseph S., *New Dimensions in Creativity,* Volumes Mark 1, Mark 2, and Mark 3. New York: Harper and Row Publishers. 1973.

Rogers, Carl R., *Freedom to Learn.* Columbus, Ohio: Merrill, 1969.

Ryan, Kevin, ed. *Don't Smile Until Christmas.* Chicago: University of Chicago Press, 1970.

Saint Exupery, Antoine de. *The Little Prince.* Translated by K. Woods. New York: Harcourt, Brace & World, 1943.

Stanish, Bob, *Sunflowering: Thinking, Feeling, Doing Activities for Creative Expression*, Carthage, Illinois: Good Apple, Inc., 1977.

Synectics Incorporated, *Making It Strange,* Books 1, 2, 3, and 4. New York: Harper and Row Publishers. 1968.

Taylor, Calvin W., (editor), *Creativity: Progress and Potential.* New York: McGraw Hill Book Company. 1964.

Torrance, E. Paul, *Guiding Creative Talent*. Englewood Cliffs New Jersey: Prentice Hall, Inc. 1962.

Torrance, E. Paul, *Rewarding Creative Behavior: Experiments in Classroom Creativity*. Englewood Cliffs, New Jersey: Prentice Hall, Inc. 1965.

Vincent, William S., *Indicators of Quality*, "Signs of Good Teaching," Institute of Administrative Research, Teachers College, New York: Columbia University. 1969.

Weinstein, G. and Fantini, Mario. *Toward Humanistic Education*. New York: Praeger, 1970.

Williams, Frank E., *Classroom Ideas for Encouraging Thinking and Feeling*. Buffalo, New York: D.O.K. Publishers, Inc. 1970.

Williams, Margery, *The Velveteen Rabbit*. Garden City, New York: Doubleday and Company, Inc. 1968.

ATS

Can you design hats
For four-legged ATS
Who are bothered so much
By troublesome gnats?
They have no hands as such;
Can you help the ATS?

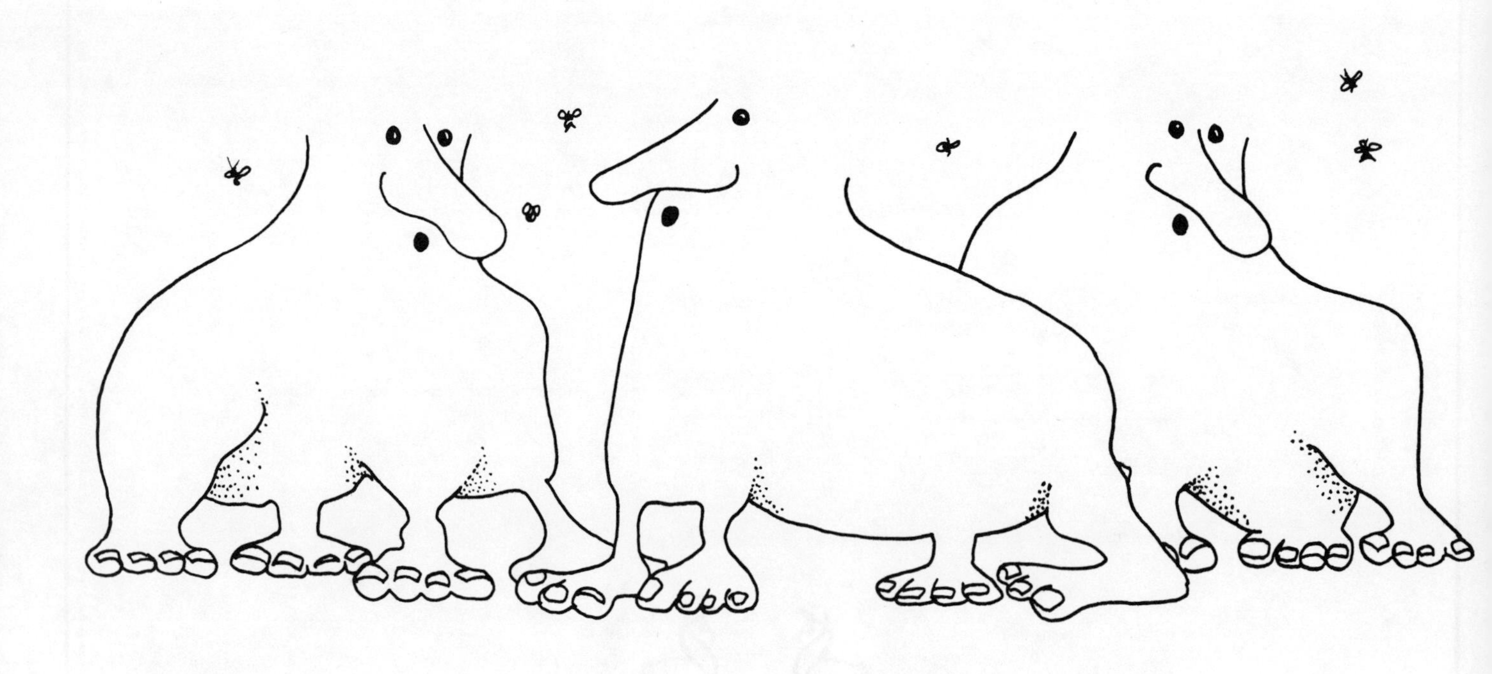

ATS

•CREATIVE THINKING SKILLS: elaboration and originality

•GETTING STARTED: There are two ways to approach this activity.

One: give minimal direction. Creative thinkers will perceive the problem and design hats with gismos for chasing away gnats. Thus, you will have a nice tool for identifying such thinkers.

Second: encourage all students to think of ways that hats can chase away gnats. Ask students to draw the hats. Give plenty of time for inventing!

•UPON COMPLETION: 1. Provide opportunity for students to show and share and explain their various hats.

2. Watch the designs yourself. Those that show special detail will point to your elaborative thinkers. Watch, as well, for the one-of-a-kind originality.

3. Talk with the group about how many different kinds of designs were invented. Exposure to many varieties will plant the seeds of original thinking later on.

•WHAT ELSE: Strengthen these skills with other inventions. Ask students to think of ways that a hammer could be improved, so that it would do more than hammer nails. Discuss or draw plans for improved hammers.

•MORE: Take the activity, centering on the ATS, in other directions. Ask the students to design no-spill glasses for these ATS without hands. Or, ask them to imagine what kinds of difficulties the ATS would have living in the students' neighborhoods. Suggest that they think of solutions for these difficulties.

CREATIVE TEACHING TIPS

When you are asking students, "What did you learn today?," apply the question to creativity activities, as well as to the traditional content areas.

UNICORNS LIKE TO NUZZLE.

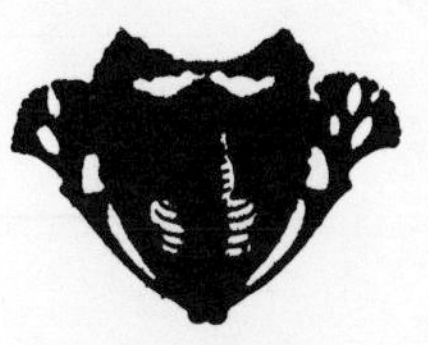

UNICORNS DO HAVE HORNS !!

What else has horns?

horn rimmed glasses

car horns

shoehorns

Mr. and Mrs. Horn

UNICORNS DO HAVE HORNS

•CREATIVE THINKING SKILLS: fluency
flexibility
originality

•GETTING STARTED:

1. Encourage students to list whatever they can think of that reminds them of horns.

2. Begin everybody at the same time. After 15 minutes stop everybody.

•UPON COMPLETION:

1. Expect a variety of horns such as animal horns, automotive or mechanical horns, or musical horns, or a horned toad, or Cape Horn, or a horn of plenty, or a hornet, or even Captain Horatio Hornblower, or whatever.

2. Notice the students who had the most horns (fluency).

Notice the students who had horns that nobody else had (originality).

Notice the students who had the greatest variety of different horns (flexibility).

3. Comment on the different kinds and categories of horns. Let them add ideas to their lists on this and other days.

•WHAT ELSE: As a class, list words that rhyme with horn. Encourage students to write a poem about a unicorn using a rhyming pattern.

•MORE: Encourage students to find another word like the word "horn," which has many uses. As a class, brainstorm all the words or phrases which contain their suggested word.

CREATIVE TEACHING TIPS

Suspend judgment during a brainstorming session. The process of creativity should be as freewheeling as a wayward kite.

a NERD SHOULD BE HEARD

There are some wonderful NERDS
Who speak mysterious words
That don't make sense
To anyone's intelligence!
Can you write some of these words?

A NERD SHOULD BE HEARD

•CREATIVE THINKING SKILLS: originality

•GETTING STARTED:

1. Begin this activity by reading a few selected limericks or silly poems. (Anything from Mother Goose to Ogden Nash and beyond will do.)

2. Encourage students to make up words for each caption. Challenge them to create words which would have the sound to match the facial expressions on the nerds. Also encourage students to repeat letters to create the proper sounds (such as is done in the example.)

3. Suggest that the last nerd is asleep. There are some interesting letter combinations that can represent dreams or snoring such as zzzzzzzzzzzzzzz or hmmmmmmmmmmmmm.

•UPON COMPLETION:

1. Ask them to share their captions and talk about the actual meaning they intended.

2. In all probability, each caption will be unique. You should have a high originality effort on this activity. Point this out to the students.

•WHAT ELSE: Encourage students to create a comic strip of characters using nonsensical words.

•MORE: As a class, create an abbreviated dictionary of 25 nonsensical words. Write definitions for each word. Try some improvisational drama with the words, letting students "act out" the meanings of the words.

CREATIVE TEACHING TIPS

The process of creativity is more important than the product. Encouragement is necessary to the process....encourage, encourage, encourage!

SUPERMACHINE

LOOK AT THIS!

HOW DOES IT WORK?

WHAT DOES IT DO?

WHAT'S BEHIND THE CLOSED DOOR?

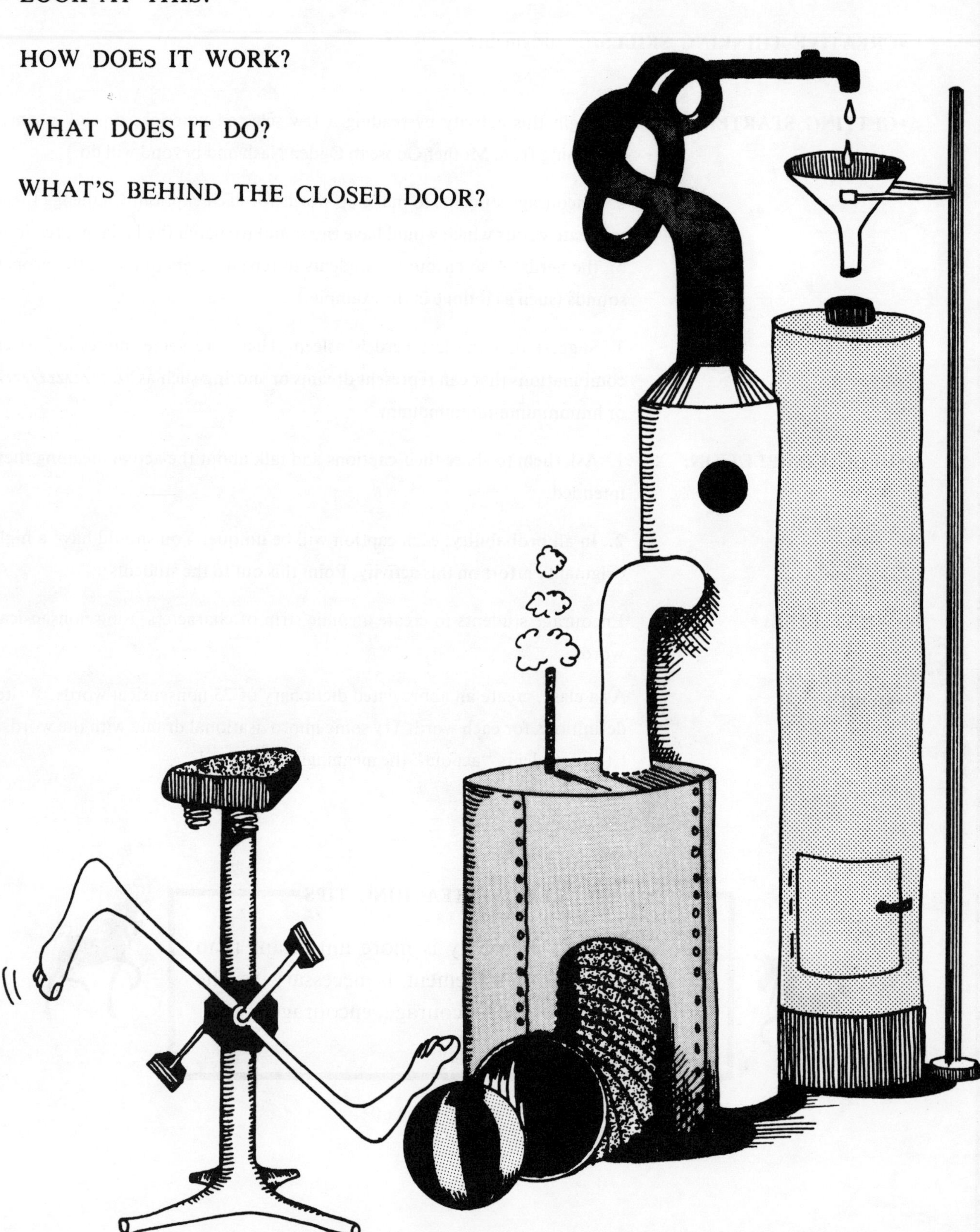

SUPERMACHINE

•GETTING STARTED: Ask students to describe how "Supermachine" works, to tell what happens to the ball, and to imagine what it might become.

•UPON COMPLETION:

1. Identify those students who embellish the operation with words (elaborative thinking.)

2. Identify original responses as to what the ball might become or what's behind the closed door.

•WHAT ELSE: Talk about recycling with students. Brainstorm ideas for recycling things that are not usually recycled.

•MORE: Reverse the procedures in the activity with suggested student additions and changes for a new fuel source. In other words, start with the door and end with the feet pedaling.

•READ: *Applied Imagination* by Alex Osborn and published by Charles Scribner's, New York, 1963.

•ONE MORE THING: Create a group collage of machine parts taken from mail order catalogs. Imagine and write the kinds of things this new machine might do.

CREATIVE TEACHING TIPS

Make an effort to use activities that promote adapting, modifying, magnifying, minifying, substituting, rearranging, reversing and combining skills for students.

My Very Own Unicorn

Each of us should have our very own special Unicorn.

In this space, draw a Unicorn that's just the way you want yours to be. Color it the colors of happiness!

MY VERY OWN UNICORN

•CREATIVE THINKING SKILLS: elaboration
originality

•GETTING STARTED:

1. Ask students to list things that are nice to touch, colors that are nice to see, and feelings that are good to feel.

2. Encourage them to think about special things and how special things can be wonderfully different. (For example, things like special clothing or toys or books can get worn out and look different from newer things. But they can remain special to us.)

3. When you distribute the activity page, encourage each student to make his/her Unicorn very special - in fact, so special that it is different from any other Unicorn.

•WHAT ELSE: Have them make lists of words that describe the special qualitities of their own Unicorns.

•MORE: Make a class collage of a Unicorn using fabrics, breakfast food and buttons, and other easy-to-find items.

•AND STILL MORE:

1. Suggest to students that they use their own Unicorn drawings as a cover for a creative writing book.

2. Read *The Velveteen Rabbit* by Margery Williams published by Doubleday and Co., Inc., Garden City, New York, 1968, to your class.

CREATIVE TEACHING TIPS

Creativity flourishes when unusual ideas, shared feelings, and the wonders of imagination can be expressed freely.

UNICORNS NEVER WEAR NAMETAGS!

Mewl on a Stool

Have you ever seen a spotted MEWL
In Istanbul at the public pool,
Taking turns on a dunking stool?
I wonder why he's not in school!

Take a close look at this Mewl on a stool.
How many other ways could he keep cool?

Cover him with ice cream.

Send him sailing on an iceberg.

MEWL ON A STOOL

•CREATIVE THINKING SKILLS: fluency
flexibility
originality

•GETTING STARTED: Encourage students to consider all ways Mewls could keep cool. Provide about 15 minutes for them to brainstorm and write their lists.

•UPON COMPLETION: Have a time for sharing responses in small groups. Ask each group to try to add 3 more ideas to the list.

•WHAT ELSE: Encourage students to imagine what kind of life Mewls lead. Tell oral stories about Mewl life.

•MORE:

1. Write a poem to go along with this imaginary creature.
2. List personality traits of Mewls.
3. List difficulties Mewls would encounter when traveling by commercial airplane.
4. List similarities and differences between Mewls and mules.
5. Create a story about a Mewl that was mistaken for a mule.

CREATIVE TEACHING TIPS

Teacher statements such as "How would you think or feel or act, if you were a .....," are cueing strategies that can trigger creative responses.

TRYING

To try as you might

Sometimes doesn't feel right.

But to the standerby.....

At least--it's a try!

List some things worth trying:

TRYING

•CREATIVE THINKING SKILL: fluency

NOTE: Although fluency is involved here, this activity mainly concentrates on feelings.

•GETTING STARTED:

1. Ask students to think about situations in which they felt like an "elephant-in-a-tree."

2. Talk with the class about times in which they had to give an effort to something, even though the results weren't good. Share your experiences too.

3. Discuss the importance of trying something that is considered important, even when you are not good enough to win.

4. Talk about "things I'm glad I've tried."

•UPON COMPLETION: Encourage students to share lists. This will give you some interesting insights into their personal values, and allows an important value sharing time for them.

•MORE: Ask students to compile a list of things they'd like to try but haven't.

CREATIVE TEACHING TIPS

Feelings are so interwoven with creative effort that to accommodate one is to accommodate the other.

UNICORNS KNOW THAT GOOD THINGS COME FROM TRYING!

THE ARN

Why does an

ARN

Yawn?

Is it because he gulps butterflies?

Does it tell you that his lessons are boring?

Or is it maybe because yawning makes his toes feel tingly?

What do you think?

THE ARN

• CREATIVE THINKING SKILLS: elaboration
originality

• GETTING STARTED: Students can imagine that there is an ARN, even though no such animal exists. Talk about the possible reasons for the ARN's yawning. You can stir their thinking, before they write their stories, by asking such questions as: "How does the yawn sound?" "What happens when an arn yawns? Do the trees quiver? Do the ants scurry?"

• UPON COMPLETION:

1. Share stories with one another. Any story that goes beyond just the concept of weariness should be considered original. Identify the original ones through sharing.
2. Watch for stories with detailed explanations of the yawning. Those will indicate elaborative thinking.

• WHAT ELSE: All animals have certain characteristics which are peculiar to their species. Encourage each student to make up his own animal and give it a peculiar characteristic. Suggest that students write a short description of the new animals.

• MORE: Discuss animals that have become extinct. Encourage students to talk about man's responsibility to all living creatures.

CREATIVE TEACHING TIPS

Kids become more efficient creatively when they understand the processes of creativity. Use the words: fluency, flexibility, elaboration and originality with students and apply the words to their work.

IF UNICORNS HAVE NO OTHER REASON TO RISE EARLY IN THE MORNING, THEY DO SO JUST TO SEE THE MORNING SUN.

A Different Beat

Fo Fum - oh hum!
This is one way
To beat a drum.

By adding a line here.
By adding a line there.
Make this drum play
In a round-about way.

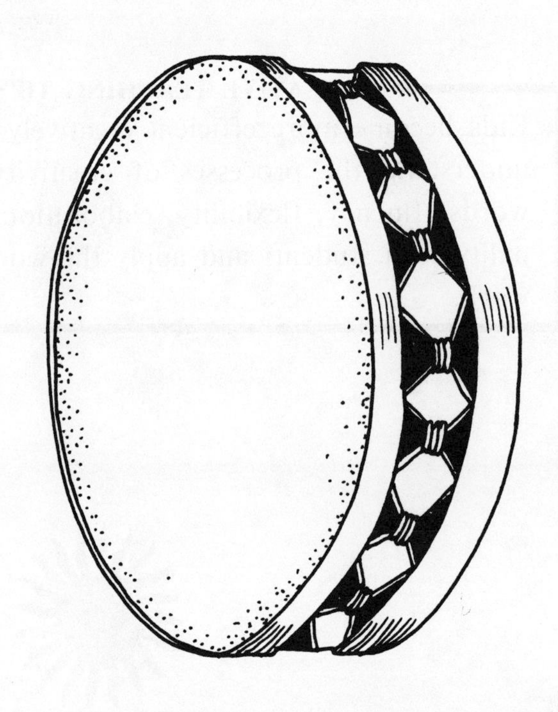

A DIFFERENT BEAT

•CREATIVE THINKING SKILL: originality

•GETTING STARTED:

1. Look at the top illustration. Talk about unusual ways to play a drum.

2. Ask students to draw or write ideas on the activity page.

•UPON COMPLETION:

1. Check for originality--anything other than a human hand, or an animal's tail, should be considered rather unique.

2. Encourage students to share their drawings or writings. Point out all the **different** and **unique** possibilities.

•WHAT ELSE:

1. Encourage students to work in small groups and come up with an assembly line arrangement of six or more devices,whose actions and reactions would cause the drum to beat.

2. Ask them to make the sounds of the different beats, using hands, mouths or other impromptu instruments.

•MORE:

This activity can lend itself to an interesting discussion on one of Newton's Laws - for every action there's a reaction. Take this principle a little further by asking students to devise a chain of events to wake them up in the morning, or to let the dog out, or to take the garbage out.

CREATIVE TEACHING TIPS

While on field trips to museums or any other place where the ingenuity of man is displayed, point out the creativeness of the products or displays to students.

Rub a Dub Dub, A Hippo in the Tub

List all the ways you can think of to get a hippopotamus out of a bathtub.

Grease the hippo with Crisco!

Lure the hippo out with a seven-decker swampburger.

RUB-A-DUB-DUB, A HIPPO IN THE TUB

•CREATIVE THINKING SKILLS: fluency
flexibility
originality

•GETTING STARTED:

1. Students will need more space for this one. So, suggest the use of the back page.
2. Give them 15-20 minutes for the activity.

•UPON COMPLETION: Encourage students to share their written responses. This can be done in small groups or as a class.

To encourage flexibility, ASK:

1. What advantages would a hippopotamus list about being a hippopotamus?
2. How would you convince a hippopotamus to cross a busy street in a hurry?

•WHAT ELSE: Encourage students to design a bathtub on paper which would please a hippopotamus.

•MORE: Write a short story about the hippopotamus who got stuck in a bathtub.

CREATIVE TEACHING TIPS

Correct mistakes of grammar and punctuation if you want to, but never place a grade on an effort designed for creative expression.

UNICORNS LIKE OPEN CLASSROOMS.

BLOBS

Blobs always feel **blahhhhhh!** A few blobs with some extra effort do become ahs. Ahs always feel **ahhhhhhhh!!**

See if you can do something with this blob to make it feel **ahhhhhhhh!!**

BLOBS

•CREATIVE THINKING SKILL: elaboration

•GETTING STARTED: Encourage students to think of things (elaborative thinking) they could add to the picture for turning a blob into an ah! Ask them to think about how the eyes, nose, mouth, arms, etc. could show "ah!"

•UPON COMPLETION: Check to see how elaborate the results are by having students explain their drawings.

•WHAT ELSE: This is a good opportunity for a discussion on feelings. Encourage students to explain how blahhhhhhhh feelings occur, and how these feelings might become ahhhhhhhhh feelings.

•MORE: Do a "happiness is ......" type of activity with students.

Example: Happiness is having a red crayon left in my crayon box at the end of the school year.

Happiness is a snow day in February.

Happiness is getting a shoe out of a boot.

etc.

CREATIVE TEACHING TIPS

Creativity is, among other things, learning to look at a thing in different ways. Every time an opportunity arises, get students looking at things from many frames of reference.

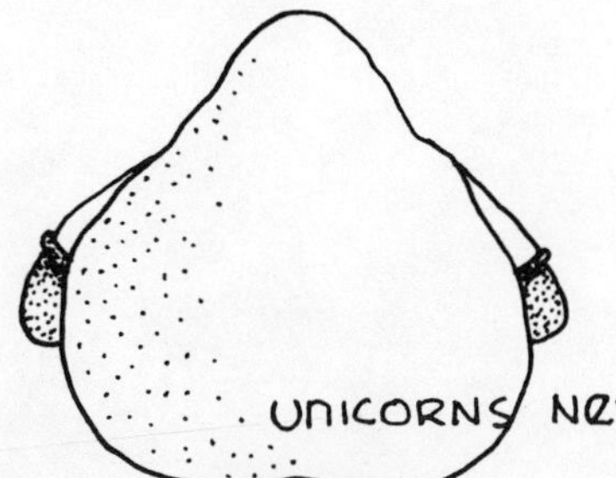

UNICORNS NEVER SEE THINGS IN THE SAME WAY TWICE.

SPLOTS

Splots are splots. See how many pictures you can make between splots. One is done for you. Splots have dots. Don't draw on a splot.

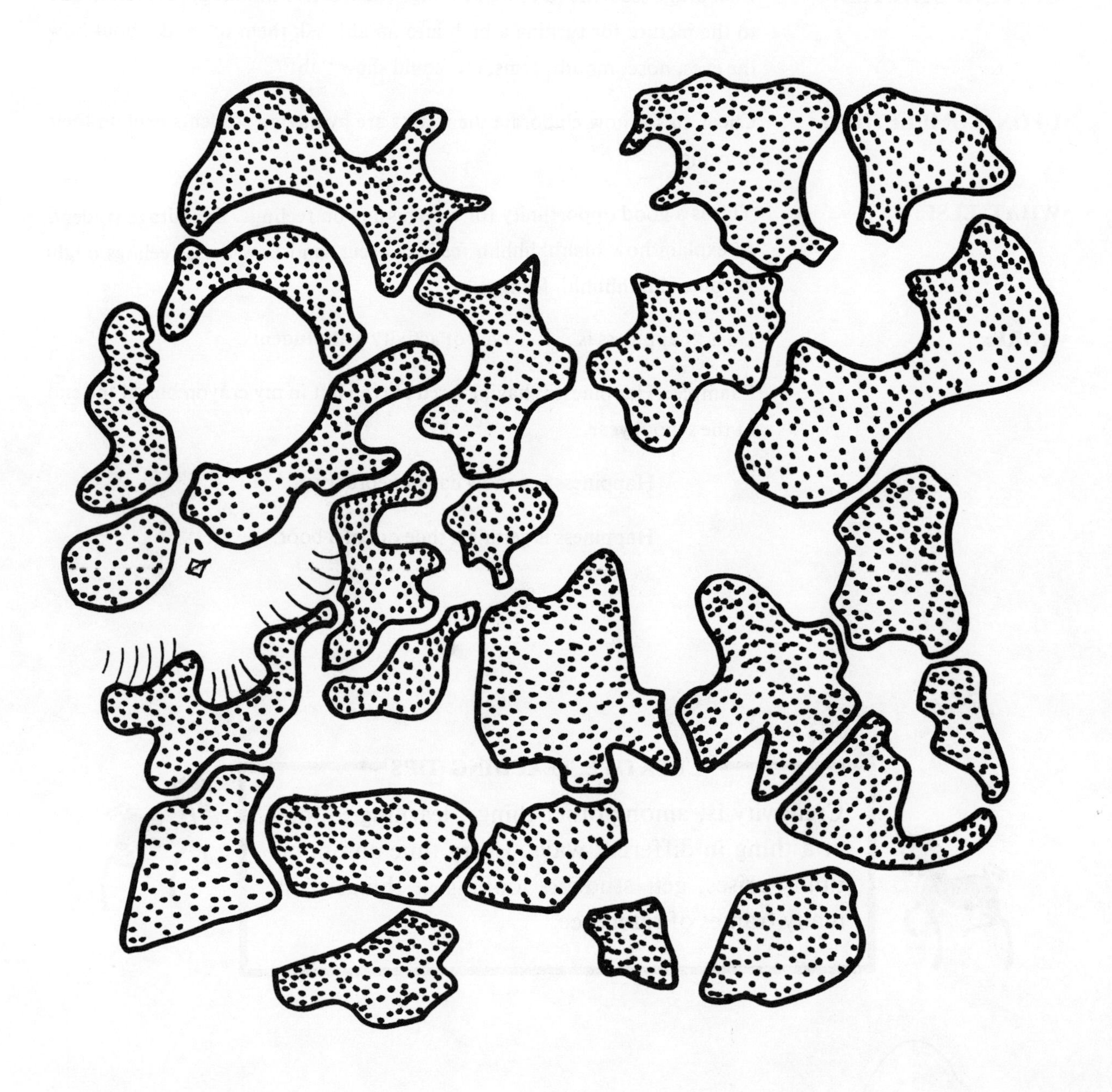

My total number of different drawings ________________

SPLOTS

•CREATIVE THINKING SKILL: flexibility

•GETTING STARTED: Distribute the activity sheet and ask students to turn their papers sideways, upside down, and right side up to examine the spaces between the splots. Tell them to look for shapes that remind them of something, and when they see one, to draw that something.

•UPON COMPLETION:

1. Have them score one point for each different picture. (If they repeat the same idea, it only counts as one point.)

2. Give them time to go back and try to add some more drawings.

3. Allow time for sharing drawings with one another, so as to demonstrate the flexibility of such an idea.

4. Suggest that they draw some splots on a blank piece of paper and trade splots with a friend. Then,they can try turning the friend's splots into more drawings.

•WHAT ELSE: Take the class outside to look at clouds. Fluffy, large clouds are the best kind for this activity. Imagine and talk about what the different cloud-shapes might be.

•MORE: Continue this activity with ink blot splots or splots made from paint or food coloring.

•ONE MORE: Make a class list of all the splots in the world. Talk about which splots are messy.

CREATIVE TEACHING TIPS

Invite students' suggestions as to means for improving school work and school life. Start a suggestion box where they may drop messages for such ideas.

UNLOAD A TOAD

If you have a toad in your pocket
And you don't want a toad in your pocket,
Could you think of some ways
To unload
A toad?
(OH...no hands allowed!)

Stand on your head!

Fill up your pocket with water!

Lean against a hot radiator!

UNLOAD A TOAD

•CREATIVE THINKING SKILLS: fluency
flexibility
originality

•GETTING STARTED:

1. Encourage students to imagine a toad in their hip pocket.
2. Ask them to think of ways to get rid of the toads without using their hands.
3. Allow 15 minutes for writing ideas.

•UPON COMPLETION: Through sharing, have students identify their one-of-a-kind responses.

•WHAT ELSE: Try a similar brainstorming approach to a common school problem, such as "How can I organize my time at home for school work?"

CREATIVE TEACHING TIPS

When designing activities for creative expression, provide a structure. Don't begin assignments by saying: "Write about something you did that's interesting." A statement like: "What would you do with a do-do bird at school?" provides needed structure.

unicorns are
having a difficult
time finding available forests.

Supermarket Secrets!

What would things say to each other in your mother's grocery bag........if they could talk?

SUPERMARKET SECRETS

•CREATIVE THINKING SKILL: originality

•GETTING STARTED:

1. Imagine together, what types of conversation grocery items would have in the sack on their way home from the grocery store.

2. Ask students to write the conversations on the activity page. Instruct them to label each "speaker" i.e. Ajax can to brussel sprouts.

•UPON COMPLETION: The scripts will probably be highly original. Enjoy the different imaginings by sharing the conversations.

•WHAT ELSE: Ask students to try this little game:

"Peek at your mother's grocery list. Make up a conversation between the items. Then, go with her to the grocery store, and see if the conversation helps you remember the items without looking at the list!"

•MORE: There are many good mnemonic devices for remembering things. See if students can suggest some clever ways for remembering math facts or other facts.

CREATIVE TEACHING TIPS

Helping students transfer a concept from one activity to another is a crucial task for a teacher. To help students make such transfers (as the association of the interconnecting threads of a spider web to an architectural design of a magnificent building), ask such questions as ... "What other things..." "In what other ways..." "Can you think of other instances where...?"

UNICORNS ARE NATURALLY GOOD AT SEEING THE RELATIONSHIPS BETWEEN THINGS.

My parents always
rant and rave
About the things
I want to save.
My room, I know,
is much too small,
And things are piled
Along every wall.
But wouldn't you think
Just for my sake,
They'd let me keep
My python snake?

THINGS WORTH SAVING:

SAVING

•CREATIVE THINKING SKILL: fluency

This activity is like the activity, "Trying," insomuch that fluency may be involved, but feelings are the most predominant factor.

•GETTING STARTED:

1. Encourage students to discuss special kinds of things they have which cannot normally be purchased. (For example: pine cones, seashells, rocks, dried flowers, special photographs, etc.)

2. Ask them to list those kinds of things, plus things that have been bought, which may have a special meaning.

•UPON COMPLETION: Provide sufficient time for sharing.

•WHAT ELSE: As a class, develop a list of things to place in a time capsule. These things should have no cost factor, and must tell people 100 years from now some important things about today's world and people.

•MORE: Make collages about "Myself" with special "no cost" things.

CREATIVE TEACHING TIPS

Make time for silent thinking by saying on occasion, "Let's consider this over a few minutes of silent thinking." Most people find it difficult to deal with silence - but it's a wonderful avenue for the organization of detail and thought.

UNICORNS ARE WORTH SAVING!

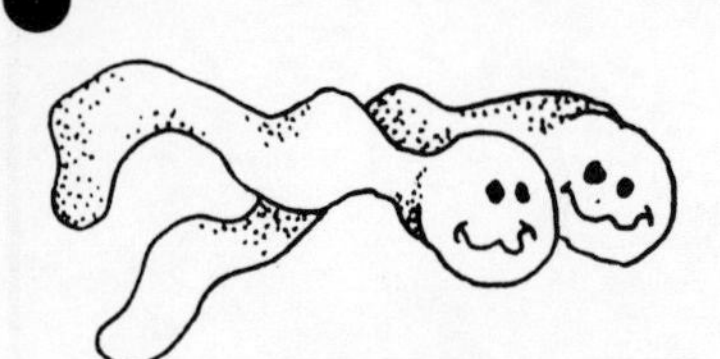

Squiggles are fun to draw. Use your wonderful imagination for each of the following:

Draw a soft fluffy squiggle.

Draw a squiggle with a stomachache.

Draw a squeezable squiggle.

Draw a happy squiggle.

Write a caption here ______________________

Now,draw a squiggle to match your caption.

Write a caption here ______________________

Now,draw a squiggle to match your caption.

My captions that nobody else had: ______________________

SQUIGGLES

•CREATIVE THINKING SKILLS: originality
elaboration

•GETTING STARTED: Most students will be able to figure out what a squiggle is. However, if help is required, share this "Squiggle with a Headache" with your class.

Another way of explaining a squiggle is to have students imagine kite string all twisted and looped together in a mess.

•UPON COMPLETION: Encourage students to compare their captions to see how original they were.

Check elaboration by identifying those with very detailed drawings.

•WHAT ELSE: Encourage students to list manmade squiggles (such as spaghetti.)

•ONE MORE: Share with your class the book *The Dot and the Line: A Romance in Lower Mathematics*, by Norton Juster, published by Random House in New York, 1963.

CREATIVE TEACHING TIPS

Create classroom strategies that will cause students to find associations with seemingly unrelated things. This is a very important skill for problem solving and creativity.

slicky-sticky

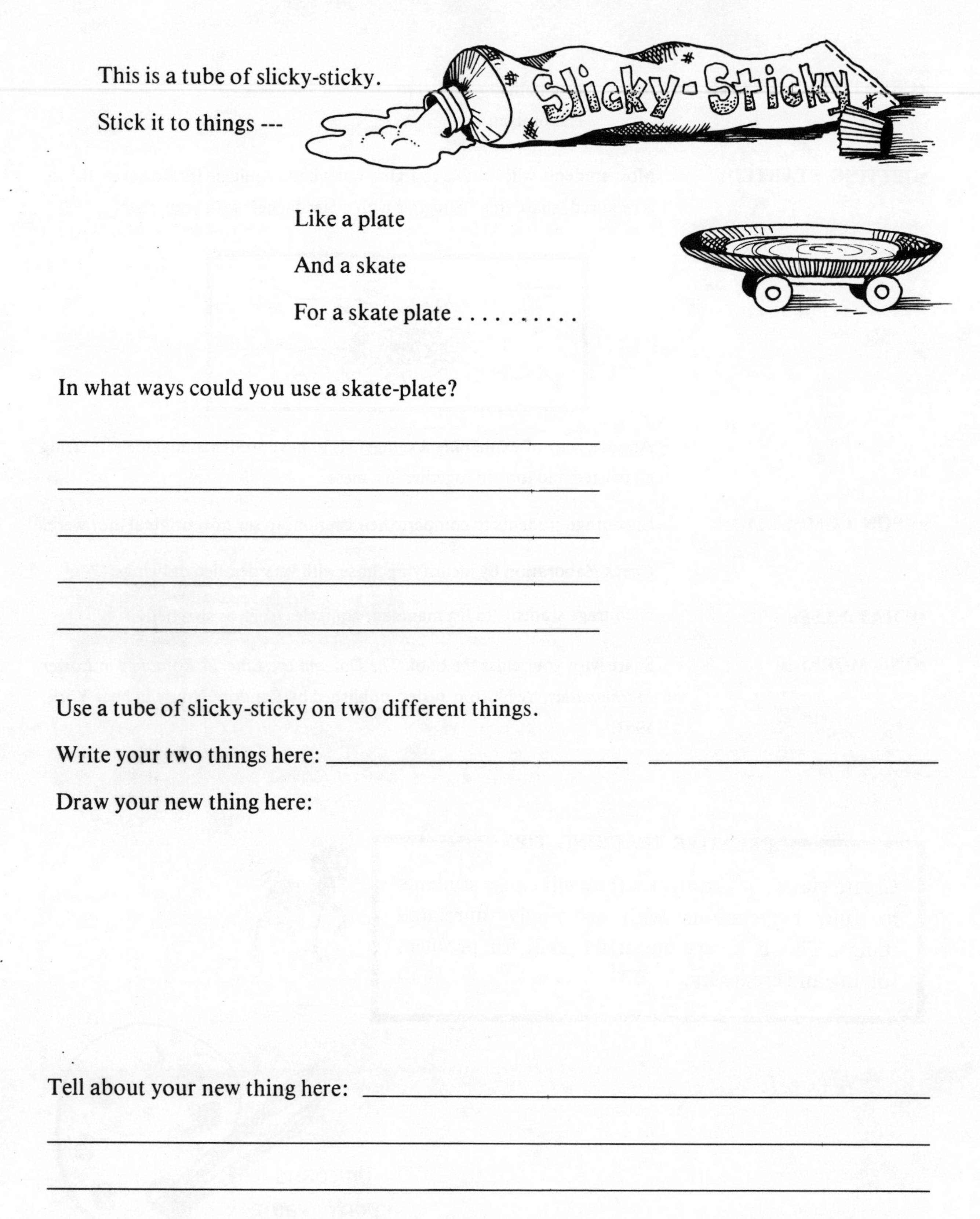

This is a tube of slicky-sticky.

Stick it to things ---

Like a plate

And a skate

For a skate plate . . . .

In what ways could you use a skate-plate?

____

____

____

____

____

Use a tube of slicky-sticky on two different things.

Write your two things here: ________________ ________________

Draw your new thing here:

Tell about your new thing here: ________________________________

____

____

____

SLICKY-STICKY

•CREATIVE THINKING SKILLS: elaboration
flexibility
originality

NOTE:

1. Should students use two vastly different items, this would qualify for flexibility. This is an exercise in "forced-relationships." What is needed are items not in association. A ball and bat are in association. A flag pole and ice cream are not.

2. Should the new product be elaborate in design and description, elaborative thinking is indicated.

3. Should the new product contain two items not used by others in the class, this indicates original thinking.

•GETTING STARTED:

1. Encourage students to think of slicky-sticky glue as a means of holding any two objects together regardless of size or weight.

2. Ask them to try sticking objects that are not often thought of together.

•UPON COMPLETION:

1. Tell students to describe in detail their new product.

2. Discuss things that might have come about when someone went through a similar process in inventing something (For example: wheelbarrow, wrist-watch, typewriter, etc.)

•WHAT ELSE: Repeat this activity frequently throughout the school year.

CREATIVE TEACHING TIPS

Provide lots of experiences in putting existing things into different patterns and combinations. There are very few examples in the world that can be described as new. What we do have are new combinations of existing products.

TO LOVE a UNICORN IS TO LOVE LIFE!

STIR A RAINBOW

1. If you could stir a rainbow, what kind of a design would you give the sky?
   Tell about it or draw it here:

2. If you could rearrange some stars for the earth to see, what would we see, both you and me?
   Tell about it or draw it here:

3. If you could touch something to make it real, what would it be for the world to see?
   Tell about it or draw it here:

STIR A RAINBOW

•CREATIVE THINKING SKILLS: elaboration

•GETTING STARTED: With very young children, encourage drawings and color, along with stories. With older students, encourage word imagery or poetic responses to the questions.

NOTE: Other skills may be at play here, especially that of originality.

•WHAT ELSE: 1. Try dropping drops of oil pigments into a clear plastic or glass container of linseed oil on an overhead projector. Encourage students to verbally respond to what kinds of things the swirling colors might suggest. Food coloring tablets in water will also work.

2. Paint pictures of "stirred rainbows."

•MORE: Make a collage of unreal things with captions about what it would feel like to be real. Use old magazine pictures and tiny inanimate objects for the collage.

•ONE MORE THING: Encourage students to write or explain what it would feel like to be a rainbow or a star.

CREATIVE TEACHING TIPS

Allowing students the flexibility of choice is important. Closure stifles creative thought.

Shhhhhhhhh and Mmmmmmmm

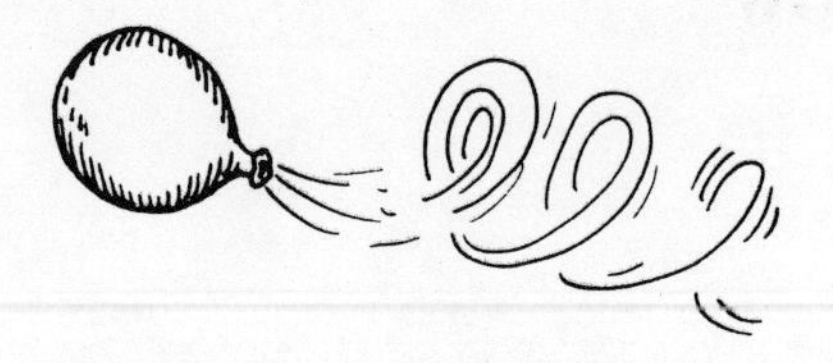

List things that go
Shhhhhhhhhh

List things that go
Mmmmmmmmmmmm

Which is quicker? A Shhhhhhhhh or A Mmmmmmmmm

Why?

Shhhhhhhhhh and Mmmmmmmmmmm

•CREATIVE THINKING SKILL: fluency

•GETTING STARTED:

1. List shh and mmm things. Should they need some help, suggest: squeaky shoes for shhh-- (A librarian would say "shhh" to someone wearing squeaky shoes.) Suggest also the sound in "shoot." Suggest candy for mmm or the motor sound in a new automobile.

2. Encourage students to study their answers before responding to the second part of the activity.

The second part is an example of a direct analogy strategy which develops creative thinking by forcing comparisons of seemingly "uncomparable" items.

•UPON COMPLETION: Provide time for students to share written responses. Let them verbalize the sounds to go along with each example.

•MORE: Try some of these:

1. Which has more fun? ______letter S ______numeral 3

   Why?

2. Which is heavier? ______yesterday ______tomorrow

   Why?

3. Which is easier to forget? ______a bad dream ______a mistake

CREATIVE TEACHING TIPS

During the ideational fluency stage of an activity, remind students to reserve judgment on an idea until all ideas have been presented.

Hurray for Homographs!

Homographs are crazy things. They are words that sound the same and are spelled the same,but have different meanings.

Try putting together homographs into a single thing. For example, take the homograph, **lock.** There is a **lock** that goes with a key and there is a **lock** of hair. Putting the two locks together might look like this:

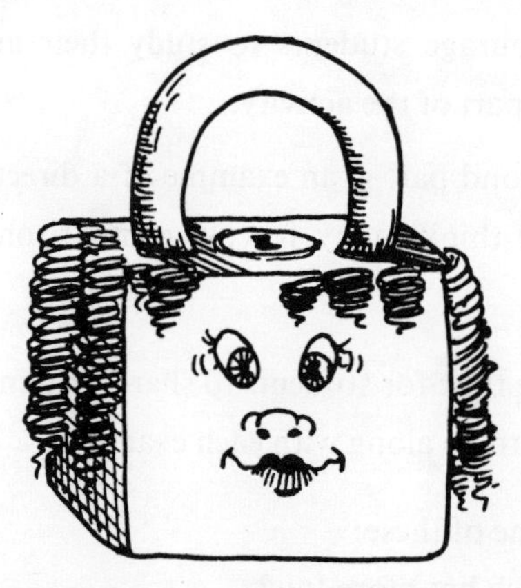

Do some homograph drawings of some of these, or think up some different ones all by yourself.

Examples: ring, fork, box, trunk

HURRAY FOR HOMOGRAPHS!

•CREATIVE THINKING SKILLS: elaboration
originality

•GETTING STARTED: 1. Encourage students to think of different meanings for the provided examples:

...a bell that rings
...finger rings

...dinner forks
...forks in the road

...to box
...a box

...an elephant's trunk
...a clothes trunk
...an automobile trunk

2. Give time for students to draw one or two of the examples, and help them think of other homographs.

•UPON COMPLETION: 1. Encourage students to share their drawings.

2. Look for highly original conceptions and those that are descriptive (elaboration.)

•WHAT ELSE: Encourage students to explain how they are like homonyms. (How many different meanings do we have as persons?)

CREATIVE TEACHING TIPS

Encourage students to find familiar things within the unfamiliar.

unicorns have beautiful auras!

Undo a Gnu

Think of ways you could undo a gnu from a canoe before he ah ah ah ah ah ah ah ah ah choos!

Write your ideas here:

Get a dragonfly to sting him!

____

____

____

____

____

____

____

UNDO A GNU

•CREATIVE THINKING SKILLS: fluency
flexibility
originality

•GETTING STARTED:

1. Encourage students to imagine that a gnu (a gnu is a large antelope) is stuck in a canoe.

2. Brainstorm ways for getting the gnu out. Ask them to write their ideas.

•UPON COMPLETION:

1. As they share, have students count the total number of ways. This will show them how fluently they have been thinking.

2. Also through sharing, note the ideas that were one-of-a-kind for originality.

•WHAT ELSE: Brainstorm a list of ideas for stopping or preventing the gnu's sneeze.

CREATIVE TEACHING TIPS

An atmosphere conducive to creative thought is one void of tension and conflict. Humor can reduce inner turmoil and unrest. You don't have to be a comedian, but do demonstrate humor openly.

LOOK AGAIN!

If you look at this carefully, you might see many different things!

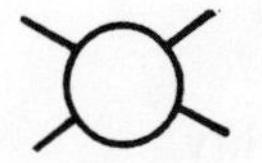

Try it from three different ways of looking.

LOOKING STRAIGHT AHEAD!	LOOKING DOWN!	LOOKING UP!
Cat with bubble gum who lost some whiskers.	A ladybug who swallowed a balloon.	Four mice in a hanging pot.

Which looking position was easiest for you? Can you think of a reason why?

LOOK AGAIN!

•CREATIVE THINKING SKILLS: fluency
flexibility
originality
elaboration

•GETTING STARTED:

1. Ask students to look at the picture from each of the 3 positions. You might suggest that they list ideas for one position at a time before concentrating on a different viewpoint.

2. Tell them to list things that come to mind and not worry about being clever.

•UPON COMPLETION:

1. Provide time for sharing ideas.

2. Encourage students to discuss the questions at the bottom. Chances are, the first viewing position will be the most popular since we are prone to view things at an eye level approach. Encourage students to look at all things from a different vantage point. This can easily be done by using our imaginations.

•WHAT ELSE:

Try taking the activity's design and having students add as many details as they can to make it something else. This add-on process will accommodate elaborative thinking.

CREATIVE TEACHING TIPS

Use the concept of reversibility often with an activity. Encourage students to view things from different positions; turn things backwards, or upside down, or reverse roles or functions.

GIVING

To really live

It's nice to give!

List things worth giving:

GIVING

• CREATIVE THINKING SKILL: fluency

NOTE: This activity is similar to activities "Trying" and "Saving," in that fluency is involved, but the feeling behaviors generated are of prime importance.

• GETTING STARTED:

1. Encourage students to think about how it feels to give something special to someone else.

2. Ask them to list things in the world worth giving. These would be special kinds of things.

• UPON COMPLETION:

1. For a value analogy, try having students circle the items on their list that are free.

Encourage students to count the number of circled items. Look closely to see how many students have circled items.

2. Encourage students to identify the most important item on their list and the second most important item.

• WHAT ELSE: Try a listing activity of things to give that have no dimensions, no weight and are invisible-(feelings, etc.)

CREATIVE TEACHING TIPS

A great deal of creative insight is associated with the kinds of questions we ask. Encourage students to ask questions that will yield data. For instance, "In what ways..." "How many other ways..." is much more productive than questions asking for a yes or no answer.

ME-VERBS

To read

Or to lead,

To dance

Or to prance,

To jump

Or to bump

A verb is whatever you might do.

List your five best verbs.

____

____

____

____

____

List your five worst verbs.

____

____

____

____

____

LIST ALL THE WAYS YOU CAN THINK OF TO TURN A WORST "ME-VERB" INTO A BEST "ME-VERB." USE THE BACK OF THIS PAGE.

ME-VERBS

•CREATIVE THINKING SKILL: fluency

•GETTING STARTED:

1. Have a general discussion or review about what verbs are.
2. Give students time to do the first part of the activity (best and worst me-verbs.)

•UPON COMPLETION:

1. Share their lists of "best verbs" and "worst verbs."
2. Talk about how they might turn a worst "me-verb" into a best "me-verb."

•WHAT ELSE:

1. Ask students to bring in snapshots of them **doing** their best "me-verbs."
2. Have a celebration each time a student can demonstrate the turning of one of the worst into a best "me-verb."

•WHAT ELSE:

Encourage students to list words in which verbs can be found (hidden verbs). For example: L<u>IS</u>T, TORPE<u>DO</u>, F<u>ACT</u>S, etc.

CREATIVE TEACHING TIPS

Openly stress with students the value of their thinking through their own ideas and supporting their own opinions. Take care not to impose your own ideas.

UNICORNS can CROSS CHaSMS IN ONE BIG LeaP.

LOOK WHOSE TALKING!

Imagine that a bug and a shoe could talk to each other. Inside each "talk balloon" write the words that the shoe or bug is saying.

LOOK WHO'S TALKING!

•CREATIVE THINKING SKILL: originality

•GETTING STARTED: Encourage students to think of a likely conversation between the bug and the shoe.

•UPON COMPLETION: Share responses and note the more unusual ones. (originality)

•WHAT ELSE: Use the activity page only as a starter for some of the following:

Have students imagine what a hammer might say to a nail.

.... imagine what a bulletin board might say to a tack.

.... imagine what a record might say to a record player.

.... imagine what teeth might say to chewing gum.

..........imagine what a doorbell might say to a finger.

.... imagine what a cloud might say to an airplane.

.... imagine what flowers might say to an earthworm.

.... imagine what an apple pie might say to a scoop of ice cream.

•MORE: Encourage pairs of students to dramatize some of the above situations.

CREATIVE TEACHING TIPS

Creativity is extremely practical. It allows us to generate solutions to problems. It also allows us to find the best option available. Use it with your class for generating options to a common problem.

Some Smet !

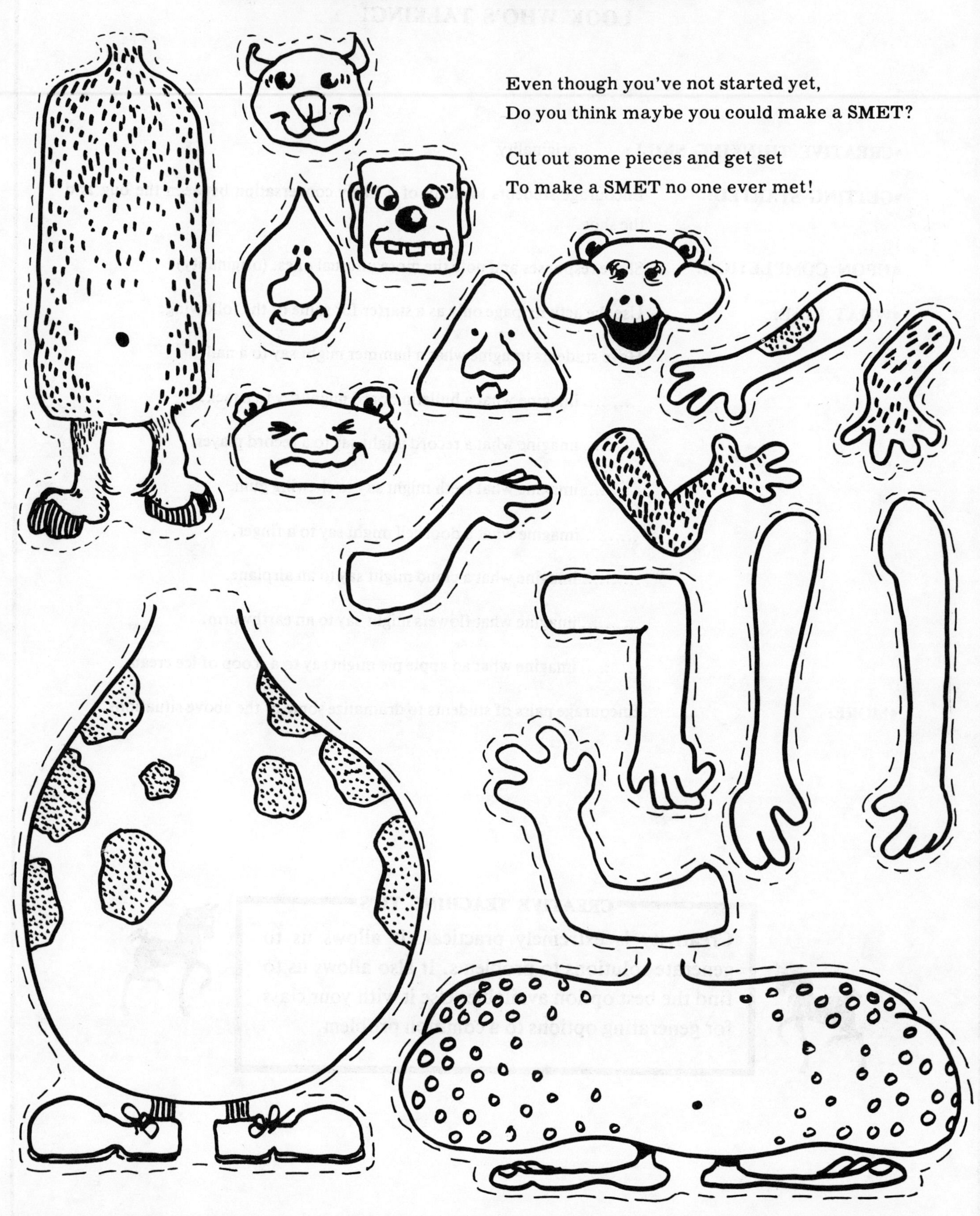

Even though you've not started yet,
Do you think maybe you could make a SMET?

Cut out some pieces and get set
To make a SMET no one ever met!

SOME SMET!

•CREATIVE THINKING SKILLS: elaboration
originality

•GETTING STARTED:

1. Encourage students to make one Smet rather than several.

2. Suggest that they add other kinds of things to their Smet (such as color or anything else they can think of to make their Smet different.)

•WHAT ELSE:

1. Ask students to write or tell their Smet's likes and dislikes.

2. Have students tell what kinds of school rules Smets would have trouble with, or describe what a Smet would do on a playground.

3. Check to see how elaborate and how original Smets become.

•MORE: Have students make up Dr. Seuss type stories with titles that mimic one of the Seuss books. (For example, *Horton Hears A Smet!*)

CREATIVE TEACHING TIPS

Activities that allow for the interchanging of component parts to create different patterns promote creative thinking.

Make Up A Hiccup

Make up

a story about the world's first

Hiccup!

MAKE-UP A HICCUP

•CREATIVE THINKING SKILLS: elaboration
originality

•GETTING STARTED:

1. This exercise in creative writing or storytelling should result in some interesting theories.
   Encourage students to think about someone never having a hiccup before and having one for the first time.

2. Ask such questions as: "How does it sound?" "What color is it?" How loud is it?" "What does a hiccup do to the air?"

•UPON COMPLETION:

1. Provide time for students to share their stories.

2. Note the ones that are detailed (for elaborative thinking) and the unusual ones (for original thinking.)

•WHAT ELSE:

Have students speculate on how the word hiccup became part of our language. Later in the year, use this idea as another exercise in creative writing or storytelling.

CREATIVE TEACHING TIPS

Show students how practical the creative thinking processes are for everyday living, by using them to solve problems in classroom life.

GOODS and BADS

List the goods and the bads about having an octopus serve as a lifeguard.

GOODS	BADS
____________________	____________________
____________________	____________________
____________________	____________________
____________________	____________________
____________________	____________________
____________________	____________________
____________________	____________________
____________________	____________________
____________________	____________________
____________________	____________________
____________________	____________________

GOODS AND BADS

•CREATIVE THINKING SKILLS: fluency
elaboration

•GETTING STARTED:

1. On the surface or even below it, this activity may appear weird - and it is! But it does employ the process of attribute listing.

2. Encourage students to list as many things as they can. Have them use additional pages if necessary.

•UPON COMPLETION:

1. As they share, determine the quantity of information given (for fluency) and how detailed the information is (for elaboration.)

2. Go back to the activity later in the day. Ask them to add more ideas.

•WHAT ELSE:

Follow the same format for information such as:

.....List the advantages and disadvantages of having our state bordered the way it is.

.....List the advantages and disadvantages of magnetic force.

.....List the advantages and disadvantages of using fractions.

•MORE:

List all the attributes of an invention, such as a light bulb, and have students try to guess what it is.

CREATIVE TEACHING TIPS

Allow students opportunities to examine things - like seashells, a piece of wood, etc., and encourage them to list as many observable traits (attributes) as possible.

Dabble, Droodle, Scrawl and Scroodle

Look at all these marvelous droodles. Add 3 scrawls or droodles of your own. NOW--turn each one into something that might be found in a mysterious forest where Unicorns live and play.

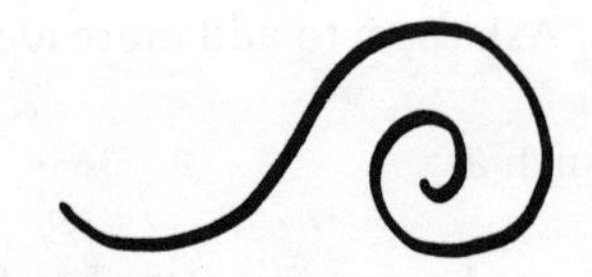

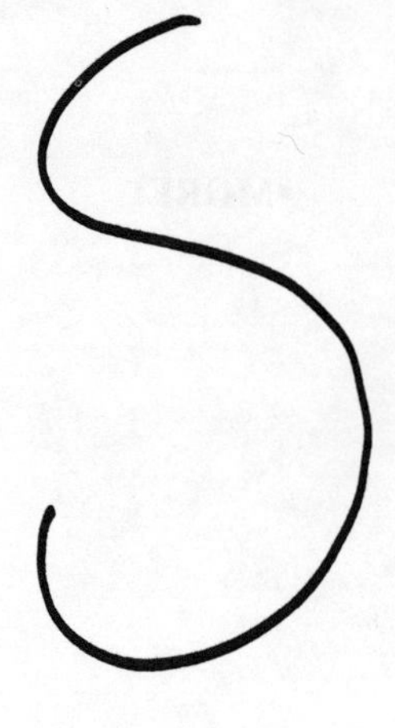

Things in my mysterious forest that nobody else had: ______________________________

____

DABBLE, DROODLE, SCRAWL AND SCROODLE

•CREATIVE THINKING SKILLS: elaboration
originality

•GETTING STARTED:

1. Tell students to think of things they would like to have in their mysterious forest.

   For example:

   .... Think of things that would be nice to see.

   .... Think of things that would be nice to taste.

   .... Think of things that would be nice to smell.

2. Encourage students to add as much detail as possible. This will promote the creative thinking skill of elaboration.

•WHAT ELSE: Have a discussion about how unicorns might live and enjoy things in the mysterious forest.

•MORE: For fun, have students imagine what a droodle would taste like if it could be tasted? Try it with smell and touch too!

•ONE MORE: Draw a droodle on the blackboard. Encourage students to list things they associate with your droodle.

CREATIVE TEACHING TIPS

Creativity is enhanced more by teacher questions that begin with - "In what other ways..." than with questions that begin and end with "Why?"

GLOCKS & CLOCKS

This GLOCK never looks at a clock.
How can he tick without a tock?

List all the ways that a GLOCK
Can tell time without a CLOCK.

GLOCKS AND CLOCKS

•CREATIVE THINKING SKILLS: fluency
flexibility
originality

•GETTING STARTED:

1. Explain to students that glocks are always on time for anything they do. They just think of other ways than looking at a clock to find what time it is.
2. Provide 15 to 20 minutes for student ideation of ways that glocks might tell time.

•UPON COMPLETION: Share and discuss the more unusual ways generated by students.

•WHAT ELSE:

1. Have students decide where they would prefer to have their hands if they were a human clock.
2. Encourage students to speculate on how their lives would be different if there was an additional 3 hours in a 24 hour day.

•MORE: Have groups design a clock face that would be attractive to youngsters their age.

CREATIVE TEACHING TIPS

Activities that call for fluency (brainstorming) will generate a greater degree of originality after the first few responses. Most initial responses are expected responses.

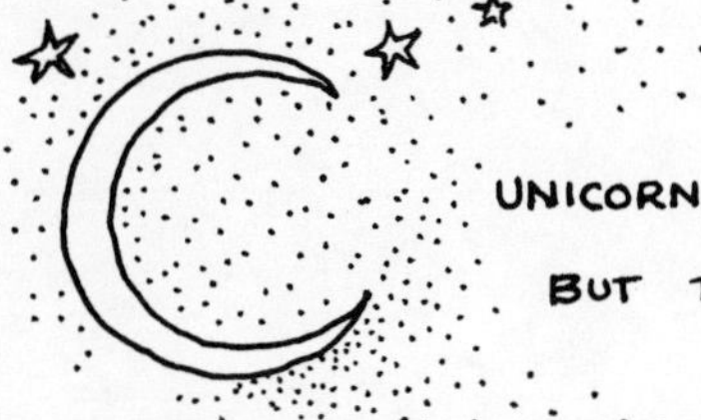

UNICORNS REMEMBER MILLIONS OF YESTERDAYS...
BUT THEY LIVE FOR TODAYS AND TOMORROWS.

Feed the Cat

1. Cut out these pictures along the dotted lines.
2. Place the pictures on your desk in such a way to help explain how a hungry cat can feed himself.
3. Try as many different ways as you can.

My total number of different ways ___________

FEED THE CAT

•CREATIVE THINKING SKILL: flexibility

•GETTING STARTED:

1. Encourage students to use all picture items.
2. After an arrangement is made, tell them to make a different arrangement.
3. Challenge students to think of as many ways as possible (flexible thinking) to feed the cat.

•UPON COMPLETION: Share the "feed the cat" arrangements with the class.

•WHAT ELSE: Tell students to think of three other items they could add to the present items. Ask them to explain how these 3 items would be used with the other items for feeding the cat.

•MORE: Think of other inventions and devices for causing a chain reaction happening.

CREATIVE TEACHING TIPS

Rearrange things so that students will have opportunities for divergent discoveries. For example, turn maps of countries upside down; reroute rivers; alter boundaries; move mountains; give a 300 year lifetime to famous leaders of the past, etc. "What if" questions resulting from the rearrangement of things can generate a great deal of creative insight and thinking.

UNICORNS ACCEPT ALL LIVING THINGS UNCONDITIONALLY!

It's a Good Day to Love a Rhino!

List all the good and loveable things about a rhinoceros that you can:

IT'S A GOOD DAY TO LOVE A RHINO!

•CREATIVE THINKING SKILLS: fluency
elaboration

NOTE: This activity is one of attribute listing - a very important concept to the development of creative thinking. Fluency and elaboration will be involved, but place primary importance on the attributes cited.

Discovering the properties or attributes of something leads to the improvement of a product (not necessarily a rhinoceros!) In other words, if one were interested in improving a screwdriver, the first step would be listing attributes of a present model.

•GETTING STARTED: Encourage students to imagine that they are rhinoceroses, and to think of all the good things about themselves.

•UPON COMPLETION: Make a composite list of things about a rhinoceros from student responses. Ask them to think about other objects that the list might describe. Ask, "How many other things are like a rhinoceros?"

MORE: Try attribute listing with almost anything (a proper noun, or a country, or a numeral, or a commercial product.)

CREATIVE TEACHING TIPS

Take advantage of natural curiosity. It is a fine beginning place for launching creative processes!

THINKING ABOUT UNICORNS IS BETTER THAN THINKING ABOUT A LOT OF OTHER THINGS!

Conversations of a Close Kind

These pictures all show things that live inside something else.

Write a funny conversation that might be going on inside each thing!

CONVERSATIONS OF A CLOSE KIND

•CREATIVE THINKING SKILLS: originality

•GETTING STARTED:

1. Encourage students to imagine what kind of a conversation these items would have if they could really talk.
2. Should students want more dialogue space, encourage them to draw the objects on single pieces of paper.

•UPON COMPLETION:

1. This is intended for humor, so enjoy the originality of the scripts.
2. Share the conversational dialogues with small groups or the entire class.

•WHAT ELSE: Brainstorm a list of other "things within things."

•MORE: Have students list things that they wouldn't normally see,but would know they're there, e.g., atoms, love, tomorrow, etc.

CREATIVE TEACHING TIPS

Periodically, do activities that call for verbal fluency, and check to see if the quantity of student responses has increased since the last time you counted.

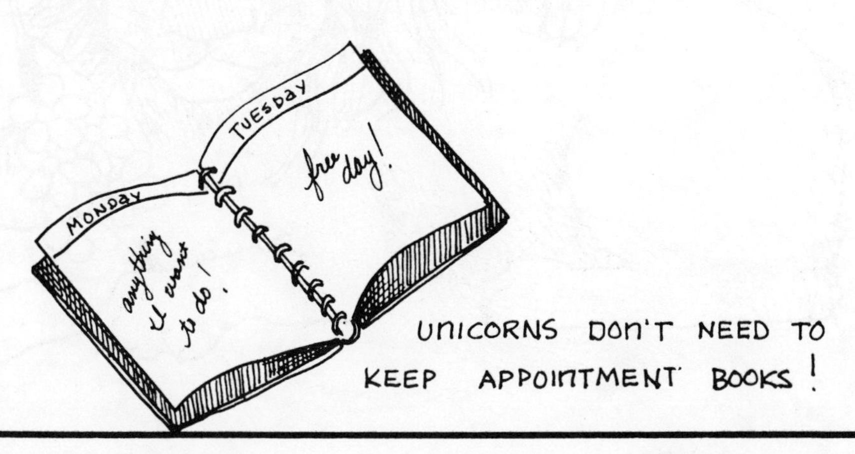

CARING

Nothing will wear

Better than care!

List things worth caring about - ____________________

CARING

•CREATIVE THINKING SKILLS: fluency

NOTE: Like the other activities of "Giving, Trying, and Saving," this activity may involve fluency, but the feeling behaviors are the main ingredient.

•GETTING STARTED:

1. Encourage students to think about the things they really care most about.
2. Discuss why it is many people will not talk about the things they care about.
3. Ask students to think about what life would be like if everyone was uncaring.
4. Ask them to star the 10 most important items on their list.

•UPON COMPLETION: It is recommended here that students share their list with you individually and not the total class. After individual sharing, encourage students to select one item from their list which they feel would or might surprise the class. Have them share the surprise items with the total class.

•WHAT ELSE: Encourage students to think of ways to say "I care" to:

.....someone disabled
.....someone elderly
.....someone who has suffered misfortune

CREATIVE TEACHING TIPS

Promoting creative development begins with accepting unconditionally the worth of an individual.

UNICORN SHADOWS

Imagine there's a unicorn shadow passing by your window. It's hard to see, but follow the horn across your page. Add some new shadows next to the old shadow for something different and new.

For an example
Look at this sample!

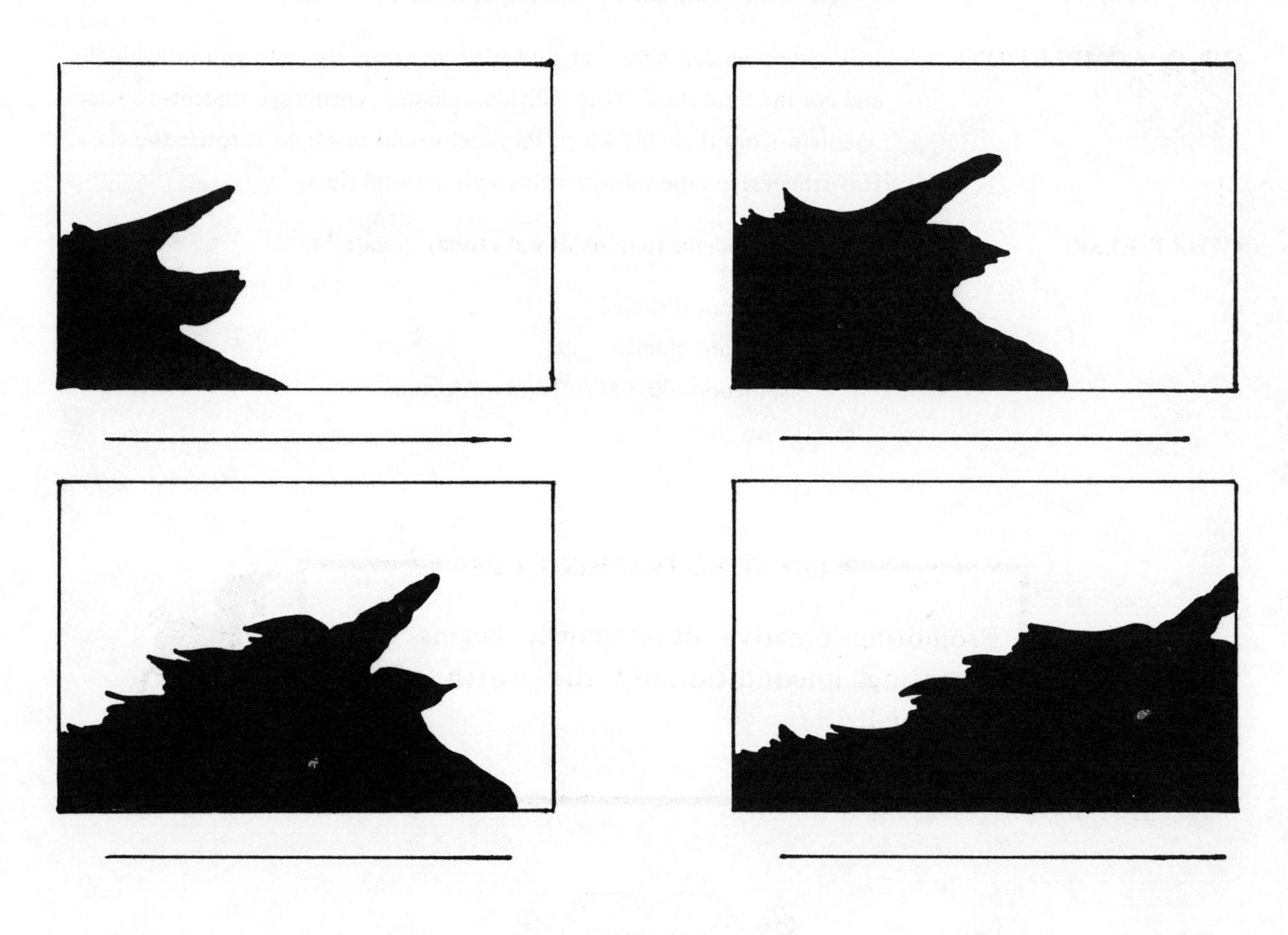

GIVE EACH SHADOW A TITLE.

My titles that nobody else had: ______________________________

____

UNICORN SHADOWS

•CREATIVE THINKING SKILLS: elaboration
originality
flexibility

•GETTING STARTED:

1. Assist students in finding the unicorn in each of the four drawings. The unicorn moves across the page from left to right.
2. Encourage students to study each picture for possibilities before they add their shadows. Should some students have difficulty, encourage them to look at the picture sideways or upside down or from an angle, until something comes to mind.
3. Some students will immediately see a face and may be inclined to use faces in all four pictures. Try and encourage them to use different ideas (for flexibility) in each picture.

•UPON COMPLETION:

1. Check those who added many details to the drawings (for elaborative thinking.)
2. Share drawings to determine those of an original caliber.

•WHAT ELSE: Encourage students to make "ink blot" designs with tempera paints by folding their art paper for a double image. After drying time, have them add lines (elaboration with crayons) for turning them into something lifelike.

•MORE: Use the lighting from an overhead projector for producing hand shadows on classroom walls. Have students create a mini-drama script for characters they can create with hand shadows.

CREATIVE TEACHING TIPS

Self-assessment by students is the most effective method of evaluation of the creative process. Encourage students to ask themselves this question during and after completion: "In what other ways could I do this, or in what other ways can I improve this?"

UNICORNS BELIEVE THAT INTELLIGENCE IS SPELLED: I-M-A-G-I-N-A-T-I-O-N.

QUACKS IN SACKS

No one seems to know

About these bashful QUACKS

Who wander to and fro

In their brown paper SACKS.

Make up a story about a very good way

To get QUACKS out of brown paper SACKS.

QUACKS IN SACKS

•CREATIVE THINKING SKILLS: elaboration
originality

•GETTING STARTED: Encourage students to think of ways in which quacks would willingly remove their sacks.

•UPON COMPLETION:

1. As they share, note the students who have embellished their stories with detail (for elaborative thinking.) Also, note those who have created very unusual ways of encouraging quacks to remove their sacks (originality).
2. This activity will provide an opportunity to discuss bashfulness. Talk about how all of us go through a period of time when we're young and this occurs. As we gain confidence in ourselves, the bashfulness normally disappears. One way to deal with being bashful is by feeling good about ourselves.

•WHAT ELSE: Interesting artwork can result by painting designs on folded paper sacks. Sack creases can give a unique effect, especially for caricature.

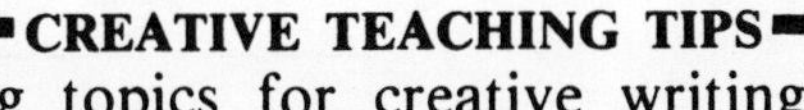

CREATIVE TEACHING TIPS

In designing topics for creative writing, choose those that allow students to connect themselves with whatever they're writing. "In what ways would I feel, think, or act if I were ..." is a type of instruction that helps students identify personally with the idea.

Color This Tender & Strong

This is a flower of tenderness.

What are the colors of tenderness?

What are some things colored tender?

Color this flower tender!

This is a tree of strength.

What are the colors of strength?

What are some things colored strong?

Color this tree strong!

How are you both tender and strong?

What colors would you use to color you?

COLOR THIS TENDER AND STRONG

•CREATIVE THINKING SKILLS: elaboration

NOTE: Although creative thinking skills will be associated with this activity, imagery and feelings will be the more predominate responses.

Do check for elaboration. See how much intensive detail some students will provide, but refrain from asking for elaborate responses.

•GETTING STARTED:

1. Do this activity in a relaxed period of the day. With younger students discuss the meanings of tenderness and strength first.
2. Encourage students to think about how colors are associated with things. (For example, warm colors are often cited with varying tones of browns and yellows; stoplights of red, associated with commands to stop; red, associated with violence; colors of blue and green and their varying tones with cool and cold; bright greens, associated with things new - like spring, etc.)
3. Then, allow time for writing answers to the questions.

CREATIVE TEACHING TIPS

Try "I think or I feel" statements following an activity. Every one begins a statement with "I think or I feel ...," then adds a few more words. This provides a short evaluation or process - which may prove interesting.

UNICORNS ARE BOTH TENDER AND STRONG!

Here are some fluffies:

Fluffies sort of look like fluffies. Some of them like to be squeezed. Some of them are nice and soft. Some of them float in the air. Some of them hate getting sticky.

Think of fluffy kinds of things and write them here:

tapioca pudding ________ puppies' ears ________ dandelion spores ________

Choose your favorite fluffy from the above and place a fluffy circle around it to make it special.

FLUFFIES

•CREATIVE THINKING SKILLS: fluency
flexibility
originality

•GETTING STARTED: Encourage students to write whatever comes to mind. Provide about 15 minutes for the activity.

•UPON COMPLETION: Allow time for students to share their ideas.

•WHAT ELSE: List fluffy kinds of experiences and feelings.

•MORE: During springtime, when dandelions turn from yellow to white, take your students outside to chase dandelion spores. Encourage students to examine them closely to see how they are structured, and how that structure allows them to float.

CREATIVE TEACHING TIPS

Creativity is easily cultivated in those classrooms that are open and informal - where opportunities exist to imagine and to express.

UNICORNS
COME IN ALL
SIZES AND COLORS!

ICKIES and UCKIES

This is an icky!

This is an ucky!

List some ickies.

List some uckies.

Combine an icky with an ucky, for an icky-ucky or combine an ucky with an icky, for an ucky-icky.

Think of things in the world that remind you of an icky-ucky or an ucky-icky.

ICKIES AND UCKIES

•CREATIVE THINKING SKILLS: fluency
flexibility
originality

•GETTING STARTED:

1. Encourage students to imagine what an "icky" is by the sound of the word. Use the same procedure for "uckies."
2. Ask students to recall experiences or feelings that would best describe icky-ucky or ucky-icky, for things in the world, that would remind them of these phrases.
3. Allow time for listing those in writing.

•UPON COMPLETION: Encourage students to share their ideas.

•WHAT ELSE: Get in small groups to talk about things that cause icky or ucky feelings.

•MORE: Icky and ucky are negative words. Encourage students to come up with other made-up words which would cause a happy feeling or thought.

CREATIVE TEACHING TIPS

When you design classroom activities to promote a high degree of fluency, you can expect a bonus of high student originality.

UNICORNS ENJOY HUMOR
BECAUSE THEY KNOW A SMILE PRECEDES
A LAUGH !!

Sounds Worth Hearing

Life is . . .

A pleasure ground

Abound with sound.

List sounds

worth

hearing:

SOUNDS WORTH HEARING

•CREATIVE THINKING SKILL: fluency

NOTE: Like the activities: "Things Beautiful, Caring, Giving, Trying and Saving," this activity will involve fluency, but the major item will be that of feelings and perceiving.

•GETTING STARTED: Encourage students to think and list sounds they enjoy hearing. Try to discourage commercial music, and encourage the sounds that abound in their world.

•UPON COMPLETION: Provide time for sharing lists.

•WHAT ELSE: Show a short nature film without a picture. Encourage students to listen intently. Then, afterwards, discuss the sounds they heard beyond the narrator's voice. Show the film again with both sight and sound.

Discuss why sound is easier to hear without sight.

•MORE: Take students on a nature field trip. Gather together by a pond, and in total silence, listen to the sounds around you.

CREATIVE TEACHING TIPS

By now, you should know who your highly creative students are. In many instances, they're not the same individuals who are high academic achievers. But, they do exceptionally well in areas where fluency, flexibility, originality and elaboration are required. Reward these students with the acknowledgment that they are unique - and wonderfully so!

UNICORNS REMEMBER MILLIONS OF YESTERDAYS, BUT THEY LIVE FOR TODAYS & TOMORROWS.

NOON IN A DRAGOOOOOOON

At noon, just imagine being swallowed up
Along with a plate, a spoon and a cup!
Tell about your afternoon
Inside the tummy of a dragoooooon.

How did you get in? How did the teeth feel? Is it dark, or cozy, or noisy? What sounds do you hear? Is there anything else in the tummy besides you? How does the dragon feel with you in his tummy? How does he look?

TELL ABOUT IT HERE:

NOON IN A DRAGOOOOOOON

•CREATIVE THINKING SKILL: elaboration

•GETTING STARTED:

1. Have students imagine what the inside of a dragon would be like from the throat to the stomach.
2. Give them plenty of time to write about the experience of being swallowed.

•UPON COMPLETON:

1. Give time for students to share their writing experiences.
2. Look for specific details (elaborative thinking.)

•WHAT ELSE: Encourage students to write or tell a story about how they got out of the dragon's stomach.

•MORE: Provide time for drawing a friendly dragon to the record "*Puff the Magic Dragon,*" as kids write.

CREATIVE TEACHING TIPS

Activities that promote creativity allow students the freedom of placing their own personalities into the exercises.

WHEN UNICORNS TRAVEL AT NIGHT, THEIR PATHS ARE LIGHTED BY FIREFLIES.

ON BECOMING REAL

If you could make this toy unicorn real........

1. What would you have it see as beauty?

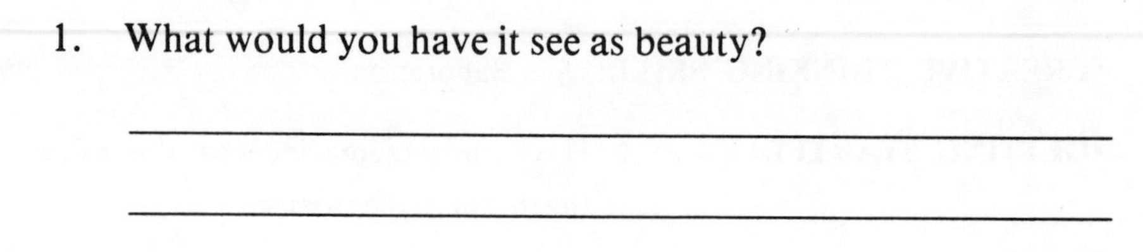

2. What kinds of feelings would you have it feel?

3. What kinds of enjoyable things would you have it enjoy?

ON BECOMING REAL

•CREATIVE THINKING SKILL: elaboration

•GETTING STARTED:

1. Should you have access to *The Velveteen Rabbit* by Margery Williams, read pages 16 and 17 to your class. (Published by Doubleday and Co., Garden City, New York, 1968.)
2. Encourage students to use the back of their activity page if more space is needed.

This activity may cause some sensitive feelings to emerge, so do provide adequate time.

•UPON COMPLETION: Check papers for the detail which is the characteristic or elaborative thinking.

•WHAT ELSE: Ask the question: "What are the colors of becoming real?" With younger students, have them color the unicorn the colors of real, as they perceive them.

•MORE: Encourage students to select 3 things in the world they wish were real.

•ONE MORE: Ask students to respond to this: "If Unicorns were real, would zoos be a good place to keep them?" "In what ways - yes, in what ways - no?"

CREATIVE TEACHING TIPS

Try integrating activities within a basic skills unit that call for student fluency, flexibility, originality and elaboration. Creativity is a process which accommodates all domains of the human intellect.

THERE REALLY ARE NO TOY UNICORNS!

PEANUT BUTTER & PORCUPINE QUILLS

A porcupine is in your school lunch box.

How can you get her out without getting stuck with those prickly quills?

List as many ways as you can invent:

___

___

___

___

___

___

___

___

___

___

___

PEANUT BUTTER AND PORCUPINE QUILLS

•CREATIVE THINKING SKILLS: fluency
flexibility
originality

•GETTING STARTED: Indicate to students that porcupines have quills, so just picking up the box isn't going to work. Provide about 15 minutes for student ideation.

•UPON COMPLETION:

1. Have students count their total number of different responses.
2. As they share responses, have students count their items that nobody else had (for originality).

•WHAT ELSE: Have students list possible uses of porcupine quills.

•MORE: Encourage students to list words that rhyme with porcupine. Use the words to write porcupine poetry.

CREATIVE TEACHING TIPS

The basic processes for dealing with humorous and fun-to-do problems are the same processes for dealing with serious problems and tasks.

Thingamajig

How many different things can this invention do?

THINGAMAJIG

•CREATIVE THINKING SKILLS: fluency
flexibility
originality

•GETTING STARTED: Provide 15 to 20 minutes for this activity and stop everyone at the same time.

•UPON COMPLETION:

1. Have students count their number of ideas (for fluency.)
2. As they share, listen for examples of originality.

•WHAT ELSE:

1. Encourage students to draw pictures of new tools which would have many different purposes.
2. Have them cut pictures from magazines to paste together into new tools.

CREATIVE TEACHING TIPS

Encourage students to role play, not only people in situations, but things in situations as well.

ALTHOUGH UNICORNS APPRECIATE ASSISTANCE, THEY REALLY PREFER DOING THINGS BY THEMSELVES.

Things Beautiful

Beauty is just a point-of-view.
For what or who depends on you.

List things beautiful: ______________________________

THINGS BEAUTIFUL

•CREATIVE THINKING SKILL: fluency

NOTE: Like the other activities of "Caring, Giving, Trying and Saving," this activity will involve fluency, but the main response will be that of feelings and attitudes.

•GETTING STARTED:

1. Encourage students to think of things they consider beautiful.
2. Keep the instructions rather limited. Leave the conception of beauty to their minds, be it things materials or things intrinsic.

•UPON COMPLETION: Arrange for students to share their list with small groups.

•WHAT ELSE: Encourage students to list things made more beautiful by age.

•MORE: Talk about what things television commercials consider beautiful.

ASK: In what ways are we influenced by advertising, concerning what is considered beautiful and what isn't?

CREATIVE TEACHING TIPS

After the completion of this program, or any program dealing with creativity, have students generate as many responses as they can to the statement: Creativity is.... This is the most effective measurement of creative materials.

Unicorn Horns

Unicorns can do many wonderful things with their horns.

Here are a few: Open soda pop cans.
Lead a few dance bands.
Steer a few wagons.
Chase away dragons.

Now let's see what you can do:

______________________	______________________
______________________	______________________
______________________	______________________
______________________	______________________
______________________	______________________
______________________	______________________
______________________	______________________
______________________	______________________
______________________	______________________
______________________	______________________

UNICORN HORNS

•CREATIVE THINKING SKILLS: fluency
flexibility
originality

•GETTING STARTED:

1. Encourage younger students to write as much as they can. Encourage older students to try some rhyme (as in the example.)
2. Begin everyone at the same time and stop after 15 minutes.

•UPON COMPLETION: During class sharing, listen for student fluency and originality.

•WHAT ELSE: Arrange students in groupings of four or five students per group. Encourage them to order their listings, so that a rhyming pattern can be created.

Ask them to think of and do an unusual presentation of their combined rhyme list to the entire class.

•MORE: Try an autoharp or piano accompaniment with some of the rhyming lists.

CREATIVE TEACHING TIPS

The process of idea production (or ideation) is one of the major building blocks of creativity.

IT WOULD BE AN UNPARDONABLE SIN TO PLACE A UNICORN IN A ZOO.

BELIEVING

Quiet walks.

Quiet dreams.

Tomorrow morns

And unicorns.

What are some things worth believing in?

BELIEVING

•CREATIVE THINKING SKILL: fluency

NOTE: Like the activities of "Things Beautiful, Caring, Giving, Trying, Saving and Sounds Worth Hearing," this activity may generate some interesting feeling responses.

•GETTING STARTED:

1. Try "I Believe in" statements as a warm-up. Have each student complete orally an "I Believe in ______________" statement for all to hear.
2. Distribute the activity and have students list those things in which they believe.

•UPON COMPLETION: Discuss how life would be different if those things listed by students were disbeliefs rather than beliefs.

•WHAT ELSE: Encourage students to bring in old shoe boxes. Ask them to go through old magazine pictures, and create a collage of pictures on the shoe box, of things that would best describe them. Inside the box, they can write about or paste pictures of things in which they believe.

•MORE: Encourage students to exchange boxes and examine the new box and the contents.

Encourage them to share something they learned about the other person from examining the belief box.

CREATIVE TEACHING TIPS

Vary your style of teaching from time to time. Allow students to vary their style of learning from time to time.

DO YOU BELIEVE IN UNICORNS?